Disney · PIXAR
BRAVE

Adapted by Elle D. Risco

Illustrated by Studio IBOIX and Maria Elena Naggi
and the Disney Storybook Artists

A GOLDEN BOOK · NEW YORK

ISBN: 978-0-7364-2918-4
randomhouse.com/kids
Printed in the United States of America
10 9 8

Long ago, in the Scottish Highlands, there was a kingdom called DunBroch. The land was ruled by King Fergus and Queen Elinor. Their sons, the triplet princes, were a trio of mischief-makers.

And then there was Merida, the princess of DunBroch.

Every day, Queen Elinor spent hour after hour teaching Merida how a princess should behave. But Merida refused to listen.

Sometimes the queen wondered how she would ever get through to her daughter.

Merida dreaded her mother's lessons.
She preferred riding her horse, Angus,
and practicing with her bow and arrows.
Merida was a skilled archer and
rarely missed a shot.

One day, Queen Elinor told her daughter it was time to follow family tradition and invite suitors from three Highland clans to compete for the princess's hand in marriage. But Merida said she wasn't ready to marry!

Queen Elinor told her a legend about an ancient prince who had refused to follow the traditions of his kingdom. He had split from his three brothers, and their kingdom had fallen. "Legends are lessons," said the queen. Merida was not convinced.

But the clans were already on their way.
A few days later, the royal family received them
in the castle's Great Hall.

Lords Macintosh, MacGuffin, and Dingwall
stepped forward to present their firstborn
sons—the suitors who would compete
for the princess's hand in the
Highland Games.

Young Macintosh was the first suitor. "With his own sword, he vanquished *one thousand* foes!" his father, Lord Macintosh, bragged.

The next suitor was Young MacGuffin. "With his bare hands, he vanquished *two thousand* foes!" his father, Lord MacGuffin, boasted.

Wee Dingwall was last. "He vanquished *ten thousand* foes single-handedly!" his father, Lord Dingwall, bluffed.

Queen Elinor outlined the rules of the Highland Games. Only the firstborn descendant of each of the clan leaders could compete for the hand of the princess. The princess herself would choose the challenge.

Merida's eyes lit up. *Firstborn?* she thought. Suddenly, she had an idea.

"I choose archery!" she cried.

The competition took place on the castle grounds that very afternoon. Young MacGuffin almost missed his target altogether.

Young Macintosh's shot was better—but his attitude was not.

Wee Dingwall was the worst archer of all. But somehow he hit the bull's-eye!

Then Merida appeared on the field.
"I am the firstborn descendant of Clan DunBroch!"
she declared. "And I'll be shooting for my own hand!"
"I forbid it!" Queen Elinor cried. But Merida ignored
her mother and took aim.

One, two, three arrows took flight—and
hit all three bull's-eyes!
Merida was thrilled—until a furious
Queen Elinor dragged her back to the castle.

"You embarrassed them!" the queen shouted at Merida when they were alone. "You embarrassed me!"

"I'll never be like you!" Merida cried angrily. She slashed the family tapestry with a sword, splitting the images of her and her mother.

Merida ran out of the castle. Sobbing, she jumped
on her horse and raced into the forest.

Soon she arrived at the mysterious Ring of Stones.
Tiny blue lights appeared, forming a trail. They seemed
to beckon Merida deeper into the forest.

The blue lights were will o' the wisps, known for leading people either to treasure—or to doom! Merida followed the wisps to a small cottage where an old woman lived. Believing the woman was a witch, Merida asked her for a spell to change her mother!

"Long ago, I met a prince," the Witch told Merida.
The prince had given the Witch a ring engraved with
two axes in exchange for a spell to give him the strength
of ten men.

The Witch set to work making the spell. When she was done, she pulled a cake from her cauldron and gave it to Merida. Clearly, the Witch was finished, for Merida soon found herself heading for home.

At the castle, Elinor was happy and relieved to see Merida. But the lords still expected an answer. Whom would the princess marry?

Merida handed her mother the cake. "I made it," she fibbed. "For you!"

After one bite of cake, the queen set down her fork. She suggested they go and settle things with the lords.

But soon the queen began to feel ill. Was the spell taking effect? Dodging King Fergus and the lords, Merida led her mother up to her room.

Queen Elinor went straight to bed.
After a few minutes, a giant bear rose from the sheets.
The queen had been transformed!
"That scaffy witch gave me a gammy spell!" Merida cried.
Elinor the bear let out an angry roar!

Downstairs, King Fergus heard the bear roar. Long ago, an evil bear called Mor'du had eaten one of the king's legs. Ever since, the king had hunted down every bear he'd come across.

And now there was a bear in his castle! King Fergus quickly gathered all the clans for a hunt.

Merida knew she had to find the Witch so she could undo the spell. She asked her brothers to distract the king so she and her mother could slip out of the castle.

The triplets used a chicken to cast the shadow of a bear on the wall! When the king saw it, he took off after the bear, leading the hunting party in the wrong direction. Merida and her mother quickly headed for the woods.

Merida led her mother to the Witch's cottage. The Witch was gone, but she had left a message in her cauldron: "Fate be changed, look inside, mend the bond torn by pride."

Suddenly, a white cloud filled the air. When it cleared, the cottage was gone. The desperate pair could find nothing to undo the spell!

The next morning, Elinor picked some berries for
breakfast and sat down to her queenly meal.
Merida decided to get them a *real* breakfast.

In a nearby stream, Merida caught a fish. She showed
Elinor how to catch fish, too, and together they played
and splashed in the river. For the first time in a long while,
mother and daughter enjoyed each other's company.

By late afternoon, Merida and Elinor had spotted a trail of wisps. They followed it through the fog to the ruins of an ancient castle, where Merida noticed a symbol of crossed axes carved into the stone.

As they looked around the ruins, Merida tumbled into the castle's throne room. There she saw a stone carving of four brothers—princes all—but the fourth brother was broken off. It was just like her mother's legend.

"Split," Merida whispered, "like the tapestry."

Merida noticed deep claw marks throughout the room.

"The strength of ten men," Merida said, recalling the Witch's words and the prince's ring with the crossed axes. "The prince became . . . Mor'du!"

Just then, Mor'du appeared!

Mor'du lunged at Merida, but the queen
pulled the princess out of his reach just in
time. Merida and her mother raced away from
the ruined castle.

At the Ring of Stones, Merida realized she had to "mend the bond torn by pride," as the Witch's message had told her. That meant returning to the castle and mending the family tapestry she had torn! Mother and daughter headed home as fast as they could.

Merida sneaked her mother into the Great Hall. The clans were brawling over Merida! Elinor hid in the shadows and coached her daughter through a speech. Merida announced, "The queen feels in her heart . . . that we should be free to follow our own hearts . . . and find love in our own time."

Moved by Merida's words, the young lords decided
that they wanted to be able to choose their own fates, too.
"That settles it!" said Lord MacGuffin. The lords
agreed that Merida and the young men should be free to
marry whomever they wished.

As soon as they could, Merida and her mother raced upstairs to get the tapestry.

Just after they entered the room, Fergus burst in—and saw the bear!

"Dad, no!" Merida cried. "It's not what you think!"

The king swung his sword. Elinor ran out the door and down the hallway. The clans chased her as she escaped from the castle.

Merida tried to explain to her father what had happened, but Fergus didn't believe her. He locked Merida in the Tapestry Room to keep her safe. Then he raced off to hunt the bear.

Meanwhile, the triplets had eaten the magic
cake and become bears, too! Merida had to fix the
tapestry to save her mother—and her brothers.
After the triplets freed their sister, they all climbed
onto Angus and raced after their mother. All the
while, Merida mended the tapestry.

Merida found the hunters at the Ring of Stones. The men had captured Elinor. "I won't let you kill my mother!" Merida cried. She swung her sword at King Fergus's wooden leg, chopping it clean off!

Suddenly, Mor'du burst into the
Ring of Stones. The clans rushed
to attack him, but they were no
match for the beast.

Mor'du quickly closed in on Merida.

Determined to protect her daughter, Elinor gathered her strength and broke free. Then she charged Mor'du.

The two bears clashed. After a fierce battle,
Elinor slammed Mor'du against a standing stone.
The great rock broke apart, crushing Mor'du.

The battle won, Merida wrapped the mended
tapestry around Elinor. But nothing happened.
"I don't care what you are," she cried. "You're
still my mum. I love you." Merida buried her face
in Elinor's fur and wept as dawn began to break.

As she wept, Merida felt a hand stroke her hair. She looked up. Her mother, back to her old self, was smiling down at her. The bond between them had been repaired. The spell was broken.

Soon Merida and Queen Elinor were spending more time together and enjoying each other's company. The queen knew Merida would marry someday—but not until she was ready. And Merida knew that she didn't want to change anything about her mother. She loved the queen just the way she was.